The Mangled Shoes

Abigail's Window

Mary Magdalina

ISBN 978-93-5559-058-9
© Mary Magdalina 2021
Published in India 2021 by Pencil

A brand of
One Point Six Technologies Pvt. Ltd.
123, Building J2, Shram Seva Premises,
Wadala Truck Terminal, Wadala (E)
Mumbai 400037, Maharashtra, INDIA
E connect@thepencilapp.com
W www.thepencilapp.com

DISCLAIMER: *This is a work of fiction. Names, characters, places, events and incidents are the products of the author's imagination. The opinions expressed in this book do not seek to reflect the views of the Publisher.*

Author biography

MARY MAGDALINA writes books, which, considering where you're reading this, makes perfect sense. she's best known for writing non-fiction, including the call of truth for which won the best Award for Best Novel. She also writes poems, on subjects ranging from personal life, Inspiring people with depression.Well...that's not less about her cause being a writer she is also a medical student from India. She knew her secret talent was writing at the time when she started writing poems for fun.She enjoys writing, as should all right-thinking people. The life of her started with up's and down's but Stood as an example for everyone.

CONTENTS

'The Mangled Shoes'

Chapter One

SUNDAY

I HAVE OFTEN thought, the best part of taking a journey was not reaching the conclusion of that journey, but everything you might achieve along the way. There are many reasons you might take that journey. One reason might be to reach a goal you have desired all your life and to achieve it lifts you higher than you have ever been before. Of course, that does not make what you achieve along the way any less important, because along the way you might make new friends you never thought you would make, see new places you have only ever dreamed of and find strength in yourself that you never imagined possible. I have just reached the end of a journey of which the conclusion was very uncertain, even though I feel as if I have only just begun on a much longer journey. Today, I have made a very important decision, it was not an easy decision to make but after everything that has happened, I think it is the right one. I feel as if my eyes have only just started to open. Like stepping from one consciousness to another, very much like being born. The decision I made is going to bring many wonderful things into my life, so I know I have made the right one. I have decided to stop living my sheltered life and explore what is outside these walls that have been created for me. At the front of our home is a wooden bench. It is not an unusual bench by any means, rather it is quite a plain wooden bench with some green mold growing on the end of the boards that the council removes yearly but grows back none-the-less. Sometimes I wish they would not clean it, because I like it, it gives it character. But that is not the reason I like the bench. The reason I like the bench is that from here I can see the world going past. I could sit here for hours watching the people pass by. Mother says I have an odd fascination with people, but people make me happy, that is the reason why it is one of my special places and I sit here often. Mother is inside fussing, that makes me nervous, so I thought it best to wait outside. It is a warm summers night; a slight breeze is blowing from the East carrying with it the rich perfume of jasmine. On some nights when the wind is blowing just right, I swear I can smell the roses from the Newtown rose garden. The night is clear, which is rare for a city night. It is often difficult to see the stars for the low-lying clouds drifting silently over the mountain range like nomads across a distant desert. The city is built on a winding range that overlooks an Eastern escarpment and one season can sometimes become four very quickly. I have longed for a clear night to enjoy the stars for longer than a few moments at a time, but I would need to leave the city to see that as the lights of the city cast a hazy dome over us all. I do sometimes catch a glimpse though, each time there is a break in the clouds I take in their beauty and that makes me happy, even if only for a short while. I was surprised when Mr Spencer knocked on our door. Mother had heard a light rapping sound and found him standing in our doorway when she went to see. He was dressed neatly in a suit and tie. Under his left arm sat a parcel wrapped carefully in brown paper and tied neatly with string. I believe Mother was not sure what to say to him because he had arrived earlier than expected. It was the first time they had met, and they hit it off right away. I even saw a silent tear in her eyes. She was happy that I was making new friends and a life of my own. Of course, she was worried for me, but I think that has already passed. I find myself feeling very nervous, but I guess that is only natural for anyone who is about to do something they have never done before. Mother told me I should not doubt my own strength after everything I have achieved on my own. She always reminds me that the strength of a woman comes from her heart not her muscles. I doubt there would be anyone that knows that better than her, because even though I know it is over, the window will be there forever, to remind me and I feel that could only be good thing. In the end that is how it must be. A constant reminder to mark the beginning of my journey and why I took the journey in the first place. Until now, I have lived as Abigail Price. Price was the name my mother took when she married my father and kept after he left. I have never lived as most other girls do. I have spent my life so far living with my mother in a large block of flats. The flat we call home belonged to my grandmother, that is my grandmother on my mothers' side of the family. We moved in here shortly after I was born. Grandmother said Father had lost his job and had moved away looking for work. I have often thought that strange as he never did come back. I was not sure what he did or what kind of work he was looking for. If I ever asked Grandmother what my father did, she would tell me, "He didn't do very much," and it was always left at that. It was Grandmother who first told me about the windows. She started to see them when she was just a young girl and it terrified her. I do not remember how old I was, but I do remember she said I was old enough to understand. I know it was a Sunday, because that was the day the Anglican Priest from Saint Luke's came and gave Grandmother mass at home, on account of she was too old to risk trying to get to the church anymore. I heard the tapping of her cane on the wooden floor as she left her room entering the hallway that separated our rooms. It was not a strange thing to hear because sometimes she would pace the hall of a nighttime complaining she could not sleep, so I was not surprised when she appeared in my doorway. It was early spring, I was daydreaming on my bed, the Eastern sun always shines through my window and across my bedroom during the morning. I just love laying there in the warmth watching the dust dancing in those golden rays like tiny angels. At that time of her life, she was hunched over terribly and used her hickory cane when she walked. She sat herself gently onto my bed and looked at me with the warmest of smiles. "Abi," she started, she looked at me momentarily with an expression warmer than that springtime sunshine that was caressing my face. She had surprisingly few wrinkles even for her age. Her glasses always hung low on her face. Her eyes which were a deep brown were focused intently on me. "You've been seeing the people in the windows, haven't you?" she asked even though she already knew the answer. She explained everything carefully and gently. Considering every word she used so l could best understand. 'At first, it came to me like these rays of sunlight coming through your window,' she held her hand up to the light as if trying to capture it, 'it's gentle and warming. It's like you've fallen asleep in a summer field and the wind that gently strokes your face wakes you from a dream you can barely remember.' She told me the windows that she saw, carried the images of people's lives, lives that were filled with sadness. Time went by and those rays of sunlight became more intense for her. They showed her images she could not block from her mind no matter how hard she tried. It terrified her until she dreaded them and dreaded closing her eyes in fear of seeing them. I guess that is something you would find hard to miss, a sleepless child. Her Grandmother found her when she had passed out from exhaustion and did for her what she did for me. She taught her how to control it. She told me 'It's like standing outside a strangers window and looking in, as long as you don't open the window, your safe, you can see but you can't be seen. There is no reason to be afraid of what you see because it is all in the past, and what is in the past cannot harm you,' she would often say when we spoke of it. Once she told me it is like ripples on a pond, you did not cast the stone, but in your mind, you can see the ripples when no one else even knows they're there.' Mother said it sometimes skips a generation and I think she was glad of that. Before Grandmother died, she told me there will be times when I will hate it and myself for having it, but I should not feel that way because it is a special blessing that God gave me for a reason and one day, I will know that reason. She also told me I was never to talk about it to anyone else even though I sometimes find it easier to think of it as a curse and not something God would bestow on me or anyone else and I think secretly Mother was glad of that also. Grandmother died when I was twelve. Mother's way of explaining that to me was 'Your Grandmother's heart ran out of ticks.' The very next day Mother cleaned her room and locked it behind her. We buried her at the Drayton Cemetery. We visit her sometimes and even though I know she is gone; I know she is still here. Sometimes when I pass by her room, I hear humming. The same humming, I heard as a little girl as I watched Grandmother brushing her hair before bedtime and when I feel afraid or maybe it is just my imagination, I hear the tapping of her cane walking up and down the hallway. Today is my eighteenth birthday, I have never had a birthday celebration or ever received fancy gifts. Mother always gives me practical things like hairbrushes, new shoes, and last birthday she even gave me a special blue dress. She took great pride in taking me to the store to purchase it. We tried on dresses all morning until she found the one she thought was just right. She had been putting money aside in a small glass jar each week with great anticipation. Even the meagre amount of two dollars was a lot for her to spare so it made her gift so much more special. When I got it home, I immediately hung it in my closet, it has hung there until today with all the drab clothes that I am told I wear. I have never worn it until today because such special things require special occasions, we never have or go on special occasions, that is not until today. There is only one thing I would wish for on my birthday and that is to see my father. Mother says it is foolish to think such things. I have only ever had vague memories of him at best. He left us when I was only young. Mother says we never really needed him because we are doing just fine the three of us. But I often think of him, and I guess that is alright. I imagine sometimes he would knock at the door. I would open it to find him standing there, a big smile covering his face beneath his dark well-groomed moustache. He would be wearing a suit and tie just for that moment. I would wrap my arms around him so he could never leave us again. The smell of cologne would hang thickly around him, and I would smell of it long after we broke our embrace. Even though I know he does not have a moustache and he probably does not even own a suit, this I know for sure because I have seen the pictures Mother keeps in a box under her bed. I think despite what Mother says she does miss him. I see her looking through the pictures sometimes. On her face an expression of such longing and I am sure broken heartedness. I guess that is alright though, after all he did break her heart. She always leaves the box there, under her bed, I am sure just for me to look at and know most things I dream about are most likely just that. Sometimes when Mother is taking her nap, I retrieve the box and take it to the kitchen table. There I go through the old pictures just to refresh my memories. They were both very young. Grandmother said they married too soon. Mother was beautiful in her wedding gown. Father was young and handsome. Mother says I am trying to create something Father never really was. I think he would say he was 8 sorry for walking away from us, I really do think he would. I would forgive him of course and wrap my arms around him. He would stay forever and yes; I do know I am being very foolish in being so sure of these things. We are very happy here. It is never lonely. There are lots of other people who share the building with us. Sometimes they come and go. We have been in the building longer than most. In number 40, that is the flat beside us closest to West Street. There lives a very nice family. The man is always polite when I pass him in the hall. He always smiles gently and says hello with a nice smile. I believe he is a night shift worker of some kind. I hear the door to their flat closing late some nights when he comes home. On the other side of us is number 44, it has been empty for some time. A much younger couple used to live there. They did not live there very long. My bedroom and theirs shared the same wall. Sometimes in the night I could hear their muffled voices, but if you put your ear to the wall just right, you could hear everything. When they first moved in, they made love very passionately and noisily almost every night. Then each time I saw her pass me in the hall, her stomach had grown a little more. Then all I heard was arguing through the walls. Most nights they argued, then I started to hear sobbing. The expression on her face always seemed so sad when I passed her. I wanted to reach out to her, to say something, anything. I never did and even now It fills my heart with sorrow. I told Mother about it; she told me to mind my own business and maybe I should have. We do not often afford ourselves many luxuries and I have often thought going to school would have been one of the greatest. After Father left and I was old enough Mother home schooled us. She had decided protecting us from the outside world was the best thing to do. I often think how wonderful it would have been to go to school.

To have friends other than Mother and Grandmother, that is not to say they are not good friends. After all Mother has been busy all morning making a cake for my birthday. It will be grand to blow out eighteen candles this year. To be around all those other children would have been even more wonderful. We did see other children, mostly at parks and the rare trips when Mother took us to the cinema at Grand Central. That is if there was something showing that Mother thought was appropriate. 9 We have never had much money to spend since Mother fell ill and had to give up her job at the dry cleaners. She does receive a small amount from Centrelink which has helped. A care worker comes sometimes to check in on her. Her name is Rose, she is very nice. She often sits with Mother and drinks tea. Rose has a set amount of time she must spend with Mother, but she always stays a little longer and they talk sometimes for hours. I believe they have become good friends on account of they are very similar. They are both working class women. Neither of them has a husband anymore and I guess they just seem to go together like the two odd socks that always turn up at the bottom of a sock draw and get rolled up together to make them fit in with the rest. It has mostly been my responsibility to take care of her since she fell ill. I think it has been hard on us both adjusting to her illness even though I believe in my heart anything can be overcome, it is just adapting to an entirely new routine and growing from there. Families get through tough times by sticking together and for the most part we have. Her biggest trouble is the standing. Because of the multiple sclerosis her legs are very weak and cannot hold her up. She spends most of her days in a wheelchair, but not for a moment has she let that derail her. When I turned seventeen, I decided I had to do more to help my family. Without Mother's permission I decided I needed to get a job. I had seen the help wanted sign in the store window numerous times when I took Mother for her walks in her wheelchair. I left home without telling Mother and walked to the small Spar grocery store that was on West Street. I unpicked the piece of paper that was taped by all four corners to the window. It came off easily enough. I stood there in front of the store with that sign in my hands feeling nervous. I looked in the window, where the sign used to be, a face stared back at me. It had been so long since I looked hard at myself in a reflection, I barely recognized the girl staring back at me. Mr Spencer would be right, he always mostly was, I looked drab. I straightened my black hair the best I could and smiled a few times for good measure. Then I heard a voice from the store doorway. 'Are you bringing that sign in or are you planning on standing there all day smiling at yourself in my window?' a voice said. That was when I first met Mr Spencer. He has a very abrupt way of speaking. He had a broom in his hand, 'here,' 10 he said and handed me the broom, 'start by sweeping the shop front, when you're done, throw that sign in the trash, I won't be needing that anymore.' And I did. I swept that concrete while Mr Spencer watched me from inside the store and from that day on I worked at the Spar store on West Street. I can honestly say that I loved my first job. Mr Spencer treated me like his own daughter, that is not to say he was not hard on me, but he was fair. He gave me my very own uniform. It was black so it suited me well. It carried the little Spar logo on the front, and I loved wearing it because for the first time I felt part of something important, even if it was only stacking shelves and cleaning. I also got to greet people every day. Mostly people smiled and took it the way it was intended but not everybody is happy or wants to be. When I told Mother about my new job, she did not take it very well at all. She was right to worry about me and I love her for that, but I stood my ground on the subject and eventually she excepted it. It was not long after I started working for Mr Spencer that Mother wheeled her chair into my room late one evening. 'You look happy Abi' she said holding her head high as if in a show of defiance, 'if you are happy, I am happy,' and the subject was never raised again. Time went by and Mr Spencer decided it was time I worked the check out. He watched over my shoulder until he was confident I would not over charge any of his customers. I got to chat with a lot of people I had never met before as I processed their groceries. It was wonderful. Sometimes people from our building would come in. Some would talk, some would not. Mr Spencer says I talk too much, I just reply, 'it's the best part of life,' and he would walk away shaking his head mumbling something about me being foolish and that would make me smile even more because I knew he did not mean any of it. It was a Wednesday afternoon when I saw the girl that I share my bedroom wall with. She walked in through the automatic doors. Her baby was near fully developed by the size of her stomach. She was wearing a loose fitted skirt that came to her knees. The shirt she wore had a red heart inside a halo printed on the front, it was stretched to breaking point. Her blond hair was tied back in a ponytail and in her eyes, I thought I caught a glimpse of someone very nearly pushed to their limit. She took one of the red hand baskets that were stored near the front door and headed down the produce isle. I watched her contentedly from the front counter. She packed some apples and bananas into the basket then disappeared down the tinned goods section. The automatic glass doors at the front of the store slid open and a teenage boy who was wearing earphones and a white cap came inside out of the heat. He brought chewing gum and a coke. When he was done, he disappeared back through the doors, out into the day. I scanned the store from the checkout looking for the girl but could not see her. She then appeared from the cold goods section and began to unload her shopping from the red basket. I watched her quietly then said 'hello,'. Her chin was nearly resting on her chest. 'How's your baby doing?' I asked, her eyes came up to meet mine without her chin moving from her chest. 'It's fine,' she replied, 'sometimes it kicks but it's been quite today.' She gently rubbed her stomach in small circles with her right hand, then raised her head, studied me for a moment then carried on with her groceries. 'I'm Abigail,' I said, 'I live in 42.' She thought for a moment, 'oh…yes, of course, I didn't recognize you,' she replied then pushed her groceries along the counter towards me, 'I'll just take these today please.' There have been many others, but it was this one that stuck in my memories the most. Mother says I should not reflect too long on any of them but that is easier said than done. I finished packing her groceries into her bags and told her the total. She fumbled through her handbag then counted small bills onto the counter. I scooped up the bills and she handed me a fist full of coins to round off. The coins felt heavy in my hands, like a dead weight, then I felt her slender fingers caress my palm. The light hit my mind like a spotlight from a freight train. It was blinding. My body jolted as if an electrical shock had passed from her to me. 'Are you alright?' I could hear the girl asking. Grandmother taught me when I was younger how to close the shutters if you see something you do not like. I saw something I did not like immediately in her window. I closed the shutters as fast as I 12 could, and the window disappeared. The light faded as the girl came back to my vision and I found myself standing at the checkout. She was staring at me with a concerned look on her face. 'I'm fine,' I said, 'It's just so very hot today.' 'It is,' she threw back as she turned and made her way toward the automatic doors. 'I'm Abi!' I said again, the words spitting from my mouth before I even knew I was going to say them. 'Yes, you told me, I'm Penny,' she said standing in the doorway, 'now we're not strangers anymore we can say hello when we pass in the hall.' 'I'd like that,' she turned and was about to leave, 'you don't have to stay you know, there are people who can help you.' She stepped through the door, turned, and looked back at me; a look of confusion etched on her face. I still see her sometimes, that is if I deliberately look into her window. I still see her body lying there. The top of her head is bleeding. Her husband, his name I never did know, he is still standing over her. The blood is still dripping from the end of that hammer in his hand. But the girl that I met, the girl that walked through those glass doors that day, I never saw again. I told Mother about what I saw as I always do. I told her I could have done more to help her. She told me, 'You tried, just be proud of that. Most things in life are already set and little you do will ever change it; your grandmother knew that.' And in many ways, she was right. The police came and took her husband away. People from the flats came out to watch as if an interesting spectacle were occurring. He was in hand cuffs being led by two policemen, he screamed and cried all the way to the police car. Penny's body was wheeled out in a black bag. Afterwards two men came and cleaned that flat from top to bottom then locked the door behind them again. Then that flat sat empty, and it is probably only people like me that know a place that something terrible has happened in should never sit empty. It swells and festers. The hurt, the anger, the betrayal. Life carried on. Penny eventually disappeared from my thoughts. I continued to love working for Mr Spencer. I met new people every day. I talked to them briefly. Sometimes I touched them. Sometimes I saw happiness, sometimes I saw sadness. I think what I really saw is the one moment in that person's life that affected them the most. I wish it could have continued along that way, but as Mother says, 'life rarely stays the same.' But on that day Mother would be right, life would never be the same again. It was a day that seemed no different to any other. I had packed shelves all morning until Mr Spencer told me to work the checkout. I never could have known or guessed that the little old man that came through the automatic doors would change my life forever. Life teaches us many things, one of those things is that people are creatures of habit. You say hello when you shake a stranger's hand for the very first time. You say hello to the person who has just rung your doorbell and you say hello to the person on the other end of the phone. Right off, in your mind, you make first impressions of those people. You form a picture of who you believe they are and that itself is perfectly fine but without even being aware of it you have made a first and a lasting impression of that person. Of course, this is only human nature or the human condition as Mother would have said, but I guess it comes right down again to human nature and that is something none of us can escape. This is something I have made a conscious effort not to do, because in a way it is being a judge, jury and executioner before that new person has even had time to show you their true colors. That is the problem with first impressions, they stick like glue, and I have never been one to judge someone new, but it is human nature to form an opinion on a first meeting. I met Himmler on that early summer's day and against my better judgement something deep inside me straight away made a first impression. He entered the store 14 and went about his business then arrived at the checkout and promptly unloaded his groceries. To any normal set of eyes there seemed nothing special about him. So, If I were to make a first impression, I would offer one on the fact that he looked about as normal as any other old man you may meet on any other given day. If I passed this man on a sidewalk, I would barely notice him. If my eyes were to drift over him, I would quickly look away because there was nothing remarkable about him, except he was wearing a pair of Heinrich Himmler glasses. The kind I had seen in books from one of my home schooling classes. But if I were to stop and engage in conversation with him, right away I would form the impression that he was just a normal old man. This man could have been anyone's grandfather, father, brother, or uncle. I would look at that man and notice right off he wore a style that would suit most old men, I guess. You know the one I mean. Long grey slacks and a checked shirt. On his head sat a Panama hat and beneath that sat the Heinrich Himmler glasses perched delicately on his thin nose. His skin was wrinkled and pale like it had not seen the sun for some time, but I would also get the impression that most old men probably do not see a lot of sun because they rarely leave their homes. That is the thing with first impressions, most often they are wrong. I do believe it was fate. It was fate that brought Himmler to my checkout on that summer's day. It was fate I was standing behind the checkout watching him, and it was fate that would bring our lives crashing together. And there I was, watching him as he concentrated on the items he was retrieving from the red shopping basket. He paused briefly to push his glass's back with his index finger then raised his head once to study me. I think it was more out of annoyance than anything else. He seemed to be hurrying. His pale blue eyes moved over me fast as if he were adapted to being cautious of people. I caught a faint aroma of spices and soap that seemed to linger in the air around him. I watched his hands as they placed each item down. I noticed his slender fingers with well-manicured nails. He wore no wedding ring or carried any indentation on his finger where one may have once been. I reached out to assist and promptly he slapped my hand away. I jumped a little with surprise. Even with the brief contact, his skin felt cold. Then the coldness seemed to attach itself to my skin. I rubbed my hand on the back of my pants as if the cold would not come off. I then used my other hand and rubbed my hands together until the skin went white. I studied it. The blood seeped back through my skin returning it to its original pink color, the warmth returned, a strange wave of relief swept over me. I looked up to apologize to Himmler. He was gone. I was surrounded by darkness, darker than I had ever seen it, a thick impenetrable darkness all around me that stopped only to meet the frame of the window I found before me. Most often when my mind connects with others there are a multitude of windows, each one would allow you to look into a multitude of people's lives. It was the contact that was the key. Like an electric current striking an arc. Once that contact was made the key was yours to come and go as you please, should you wish. I stepped to the window. The room was empty. The decor was of a different time. Old wooden toys sat on a shelf along the far wall. A single bed was set back into one corner, it was made neatly with a teddy bear dressed in a school uniform resting against the pillows. The walls were covered with wallpaper displaying tiny little drummer boys on parade. It was a room perfectly set for any small boy. In the center of the wall, opposite the book shelve, hung a large picture in a heavy timber frame and protected by a sheet of glass. My eyes were drawn to it. It was a setting of some far away jungle painted in oil paint. A green mass of giant trees spread across the canvas. Vines hung from the large limbs. Ferns and small palms covered the undergrowth. Even from across the room I could see the faint brush strokes. It was a beautiful picture. The picture did not seem out of place but perfect for a boy's bedroom wall I would suppose. It was a picture that would cultivate any boy's imagination, filling it with wonder and the promise of adventure. It held my attention as if on purpose. The darkness and shadows within the painting seemed to call to me. 'Come closer Abigale and I'll tell you my secret', like a spider to a fly. Maybe it was the narrow path that led into the jungle and disappeared into the darkness of the undergrowth. I think perhaps it was the dark hiding spots under the trees and the palms that could hold something a boy's imagination could give birth to, as there would be in any jungle. The darkness also held the promise of terror and within my mind it seemed to call all my attention. I found myself staring at it until my eyes hurt, until I was sure there was something staring back and that, I believe was what the artist was trying to achieve. Then I was sure I could see it. Two faint red eyes hiding in the darkness and a faint growl like distant thunder on a clear summers day or maybe my imagination put them there and they were never really there at all. No, I was sure of it. At the end of the path that was swallowed by darkness there was two faint red dots I could only guess could be eyes. Then I could not see them at all. My eyes watered. I rubbed them until they cleared. I had lost them in the darkness straining my eyes to see them. Then the bedroom door opened, and a small blonde-haired boy ran into the room. He was dressed only in pajama pants. He went straight to the window. He grabbed hold of the brass latch that kept the windows shut. He pulled at them with all his might until I could see the white bones of his hands, but they would not budge. He was crying with such deep body shaking sobs. He beat at the window with his fists until I thought the glass would shatter. Inside his eyes I saw terror I had never witnessed before. Something caught his attention from the doorway. Something was coming. He turned to face it. I could see the shadows dancing along the hallway. Slow and menacing. A dark mass threatening to form into any number of monsters that could live inside a fearstricken mind. It came closer. The boy backed up against the window. I held my hand against the cold glass, but his bare skin failed to warm it. Closer it came until the shadows reached the doorway. The shadows grew longer and took shape. The dark mass grew arms and a head formed where once only darkness dwelled. I was sure it had changed to a form the boy knew only too well. A creature to be feared, just for him. A man came around the edge of the open door. A very neatly dressed man of around middle age. He had a very pale complexion; he was sweeting and his skin looked like the contents of the lard tin Mother keeps inside the fridge and that is when I first met Mr Lard He was dressed as if he worked in an office. He was wearing a suit, the kind a cashier might wear, except this suit had a large patch of blood smeared across the front where his heart would be beating. Casually the man walked into the boy's bedroom. He removed his suit coat and laid it out on the boy's bed as if being very careful not to wrinkle it. He studied the coat for a moment then reached out and plucked a loose thread from it, discarded it, and smoothed it with the back of his hand as if the blood were of little concern to him. The boy turned back to the window. His face was against the glass. He screamed for help with a silent voice. I wanted to help him, I wanted to tell him not to be afraid, that everything was going to be alright. But it was not going to be alright, because I was not really even there, and neither were they. Just a reflection of something that once happened. Like Grandmother said just like throwing stones into a pond, the ripple goes on and on. He stood over the boy silently, the boy stared up at him gently shaking his head, he repeated the words 'no', over and over. Even without being able to hear the words everyone knows what no looks like coming from silent lips. He then removed his belt. Ever since that moment I have hated the number seven. That is the number of times he hit that boy with that belt. I felt every strike of the leather, from one through to seven and when it was done, I hated that man with all the hate I could muster, whoever he was. When he was done, he replaced his belt and lowered himself to one knee. He hugged that boy as tenderly as any loving father could, then with his hand he gently stroked the boy's hair away from his face. I could not understand what he was saying to the boy, but the words did nothing to relieve the boys fear. He then stood up, put his coat on and left the room as if he had never been there. Before the door bolt even had time to engage a voice cut through the darkness behind me, 'Young lady are you alright?' The warm summer day flooded back into my vision with a wave of brightness. Mr Spencer was standing with Himmler looking at me. I held a milk bottle in my hand. A large pool of white liquid covered the checkout. I must have busted the milk bottle when I was looking through the window. Then Mr Spencer's hand was on my shoulder, 'Abigale, what happened?' he asked. 'I… I don't know,' I managed to say. I did not realize my face was wet with tears. I wiped at them with the back of my hands. I had never seen Mr Spencer that mad before. He helped the old man with his grocery's and walked him to the door with a wave of apologies. I fetched a cleaning bucket and wiped up the spilt milk. Mr Spencer did not stay mad long, he never does. After I had been to the bathroom and cleaned up my face, he came to me with all the concern any father would have for his own daughter. He told me he was very worried about me and that I must be coming down with something serious. He sent me home for the remainder of the day. He even called mother to make sure I got home alright. I walked home with the sunshine on my face, and I felt better, but the boy lingered deeply in my thoughts.

MONDAY

That night sleep eluded me with an unending determination. I slipped in and out of sleep as I lay on my bed gazing out through my window. Low lying clouds drifted past on the Eastern breeze. Each time I shut my eyes, I saw the boy, he seemed to invade that dark space that exists between sleep and awake. Each time I dozed, the ripples that I saw that day forced my eye lids to spring open like tightly coiled springs. The time was two hours past midnight. I know this because the Reaper told me. That is the old clock that sits in the hallway. It sounded off two chimes. Ever since Mother and I moved in with Grandmother and I heard that clock for the first time I have hated it. It could only be a child that could conjure up such images of the Reaper himself ringing his death bell, and to a young girl it was the most terrifying sound in the world especially in the dark and emptiness of the night. The chimes echoed throughout the house, filling every dark corner. I lay awake feeling as if in a dream state. Even though it was a warm January night I pulled the bed covers up around my neck. The house was silent. My fists filled with bed covers and I held them hard to my throat until I felt my skin begin to perspire. I lowered the covers enough so I could peer over them and see the entirety of my room.

I scanned the room from side to side. Darkness filled it. I saw shadow drenched corners. In the corner beside my dresser was my wardrobe with the door open ever so slightly. I imagined leathery fingers creeping out from the darkness but pushed the thought away. I searched the pile of cloths on the chair in the corner, they were all hiding places for anything that preferred the darkness to light. For the thing that calls the darkness home, it would always linger there, watching, waiting to slither into my room from one dark place to the next. One dark doorway would open into another, and it could be in my room. It could be under my bed, in my wardrobe or any of the dark shapes that stop being familiar belongings to me once the lights are turned out. Of course, the house is not completely dark. In the hallway are senser lights that light up when movement is detected. Rose had had a maintenance man that worked for the home help company come and install them for if Mother should need to use the bathroom during the night. I suddenly felt a strong breeze blow through my window gently caressing my face. It felt cooling against the perspiration that was growing on my face from the heat beneath the covers. I would not move them though, if something were to come from the darkness, I would be ready, without them I would be vulnerable even though my arms and legs felt paralyzed under the weight of them. I then heard a familiar tapping sound coming from far down the hallway. I held my breath and listened until I was certain I could hear my own heart beating. Another tap came, it was faint, like a single raindrop falling onto the roof. It started as one, then another until it became a storm, pouring down the hallway in a torrent. Something deep inside myself told me it was only Grandmother's cane on the wooden floorboards. It was a comforting sound. As I lay there, I started to repeat the words in my head, 'I am not afraid, I am not afraid,' until I convinced myself I had nothing to fear, or I had nothing to fear of what my mind may put there. I had known the sound of Grandmothers cane since I was a little girl and at that moment began to relish with anticipation the thought of seeing her warm face greet me from around the doorway. The sound quickly grew louder, each tap hitting my head like a hammer. The sound made my headache, it was agonizing. I thought I was going to pass out. My eyes began to grow heavy as if tiny hands were pushing them shut, I resisted with all my might. I struggled with all my will to keep my eyes open until the muscles in my face began to burn. I was losing the struggle. It was a safe sound, although a terrible sound, a sound impossible to fight but I would not let it win, I could not. I tried to concentrate my remaining consciousness on the tapping sound coming along the hallway. In my mind I reached for it. That sound was a safe sound, it was a home sound. Grandmother would come around the doorway and fill my mind with love and warmth and all the dark shadows would disappear. The tapping grew louder as if too loud to be an old lady with arteritis in both hands anymore. It grew louder. It filled my head, drowning out all my thoughts like that death bell calling out its last warning. It was almost at the door. I struggled to lift my head. I had to watch the doorway. My eyes were unbearably heavy, they were going to close before she reached my door and whatever was coming would come around the doorway and make known it's intent. But these thoughts were wrong, Grandmother was not going to come around the doorway, Grandmother was dead. The spring suddenly let go and my eyes opened wide. I struggled to lift my arms and legs, they remained frozen. I stared down my nose, too afraid to take my eyes from the doorway. My heart was beating hard in my chest. My body began to tremble. A dark shape appeared at the edge of the door frame. At that moment I wished those sensor lights would come on and chase away the darkness. The shape lingered on the edge of the door frame. I lifted my head with all my will as the boy from the window stepped into the doorway. Fear gripped itself onto my body. All I could do was lay there as the boy stood in the doorway staring at me, a strange confident grin covered his young face. The boy had a firm grip on Grandmother's cane as if holding it in triumphant victory. He deliberately held it in front of himself. He wanted me to see it, to display it. He was still only dressed in his pajama bottoms. His blond hair was neatly parted. His blue eyes seemed overly bright like two jewels had been placed there instead of eyes. On his upper arms I could see the fresh welts from the beating the man had given him when I was watching him through the window earlier that day. I tried to speak, my mouth was paralyzed, only air came out of the corner of my mouth in a light whistling sound like a child trying to blow out a candle. I struggled to open my mouth, to scream, to tell it to go back where it came from. The boys smile widened as he watched me trying to resist. His stomach heaved inwards sharply as a chuckle crept up from the bottom of his stomach to his mouth and escaped past his thin pale lips. I watched the boy as he lent on Grandmother's cane for support then erupted into a fit of laughter watching me struggling. It was then the fear released its grip on my jaw and a scream made its way up my throat like a black rat crawling from its hole, it crossed my tongue and met the hand that suddenly came from the darkness clamping across my mouth like a vice. The hand was warm and soft, it carried the smell of Grandmother which was filling my senses. A rich sweat fragrance seeped into the room like ghostly fingers grabbing hold of everything in its path, it filled my nostrils, it was so familiar, it relaxed me, my heartbeat slowed with my breathing. I looked towards the door over the hand covering my mouth, the boy was gone. "Abi honey?" a voice whispered gently into my ear. I felt the warm breath with each word, "try to remember, the boy is just a ripple on a pond, you don't have to be afraid of him, but the beast is hungry." It was then that the sensor lights in the hallway flashed on chasing away the darkness from my room. I lay still in my bed as I watched Mother wheel her chair into my doorway. She sat there momentarily then wheeled into my room to my bed. I never moved a muscle as she pulled the covers back from my sweating body leaving my bare skin to enjoy the refreshing breeze that was coming through my window. She then disappeared back into the hallway. The Reaper called out that it was three hours past midnight as I lay there staring out at the clouds. I could not help but think of Grandmother and the boy as sleep quickly consumed me and as the last ounce of fight went out of my body, I remembered the source of the fragrance that filled my room, and it was that thought that filled me with happiness and hope as I slipped into sleep. My tired eyes opened to bursts of sunlight flooding in from my window. I rubbed them with the back of my hand, pushing away what sleep remained. A single Blue Wren was sitting on my windowsill. The tiny black feathers of its tail waved around franticly as it danced its little dance for me right there on my windowsill. The bright blue feathers that adorned its head seemed loud against its very small size. I laid there transfixed by it. It seemed as magical as any fairy from any magical place where such things as fairy's would exist and dance away their cares in endless summer days filled with nothing but happiness. I heard a dull thumping noise coming from outside of our flat. I listened. The sound was coming from the stairwell. If you entered the building and wanted to reach the different levels, you would need to use it. If you were to use the stairwell it would lead you to the hallways that divided the flats. The Blue Wren took to flight at the sound and disappeared from sight. I was sad to see it go. Then came more thumping noises. I sat up and listened. Sometimes you would hear people in the hall coming and going at all hours of the day and night. Sometimes people would be talking or laughing. The Italian gentleman who lives at the end of the hall in unit 50 sings quietly to himself. I believe he thinks he sings quietly to himself. He always sings in Italian, and I do not understand a word he says but I can hear it from my room, and it always makes me happy, and I guess you could put any words to the song you chose. The noise grew louder and got the best of my curiosity. I jumped from my bed and hurried out of my room. Mother's door was closed, it would be some time before Mother rose for the day. I left the hall and entered the kitchen. The front door was on the opposite side of the kitchen. The noise had stopped. I reached the door and disengaged the large bolt lock that was just above the door handle and threw open the door as the source of the noise was passing our doorway. It was Himmler, the man I had served in the store the previous day. He was already disappearing down the hall as I opened ours. I remained silent so not to draw his attention. He did not notice that I was watching him from our doorway. He was returning from somewhere he had been, and the source of the thumping noise was being dragged behind him. It was a tug-a-long trolly. It was not anything special but a normal everyday trolly you would buy from any of the cheap shops that traded around Toowoomba. It was covered in a red and black tartan pattern. I do remember that it looked heavy, as I could see him straining slightly to pull it and the tiny axle was slightly bent under the weight. I watched him as he reached flat 48. He stood the trolly up and proceeded to search through his pockets then produced a key that he slipped into the flat's keyhole. Without glancing sideways, he pulled the trolly across the threshold and closed the door behind him. I left for work early that day, even before Mother had even risen. That summers day was a day that most people in the city of Toowoomba would never forget. It was as if a curtain had been closed over the city, filling it with darkness. It would be some time before it would be parted to let the sunshine back in. That is the funny thing about darkness, for darkness to disappear all you really need is a single spark, the spark would soon become a fire storm and change everything in its path, but for the moment that spark was only smoldering. I enjoyed my walk to the store that morning. My eyes felt heavy from the previous night, but I felt reenergized, like someone waking from a deep sleep I suppose. Everything that I saw that morning seemed to amaze me. The trees that lined the street, the way the leaves crunched under my feet. The early morning buses rushed past carrying commuters to their jobs or to school. I thought about that briefly, what type of jobs would those people do, I guess they would all do exciting jobs, jobs that made them as happy as I felt that morning, but that was unrealistic, the world was not always a happy place and people were not always happy in their jobs or their life. I was enjoying my walk so much that I did not notice a lady jogger approaching me. She brushed passed me nearly knocking me over then disappeared onto West Street. I stood there on the footpath for a moment and watched her disappear without even an acknowledgement that she almost knocked me over, but I did not let it dampen my mood. I reached the store in the same mood I left home that morning, the jogger already fading from my thoughts. Mr Spencer was already busy putting out the displays. The small delivery truck that delivers the Toowoomba Chronicle had already thrown the bundles from the back of the truck and left. The papers sat to the left of the automatic doors. The three piles of newspapers were each tied neatly with thin blue strapping. Normally Mr Spencer would have already taken the papers in and placed them near the paper racks to be unpacked. He stood and watched me approaching. He had the same look of concern on his face he had the previous day. I slipped my hand beneath the blue strapping of the first bundle of papers. I picked it up and carried it towards the front door. The strapping was cutting into my finger by the time I reached the paper rack. Mr Spencer continued to watch me even though his concerned expression had changed to a warm smile. I knew he was happy to see me again. I sat the papers down near the paper rack. I grabbed the loose piece of strapping on the bundle and with a quick pull it snapped and released the papers. I picked up the first bundle and placed them in the paper rack when Mr Spencer came in through the front entrance. The store was open for the day. I guess it was at that moment that those curtains closed completely blocking out all rays of sunshine. On the front page was a picture of a young boy. A blond-haired boy with deep blue eyes. The boy I had seen receiving seven whips from a leather belt. The picture did not reveal what he was doing when that picture was taken, but he looked happy. He was probably on a family outing or at home playing with brothers or sisters, or even playing catch with his father and his mother happened to take his picture at a happy moment in his young life. It said his name was Danny Williams. His body had been found in the small Creek that ran the length of the mountain that the city was built on. Danny was the first of the missing children and unfortunately for his family that picture was probably the last happy moment they had together. That day passed uneventfully even though I caught Mr Spencer watching me from the service counter on several occasions. It did make me feel glad that he was so concerned about my welfare, and I love him for that. I kept myself busy with serving customers, cleaned and stacked shelves but I found my thoughts lingered on Grandmother and by the days end I found it hard to think of anything else. That afternoon I waited eagerly for the last customer to pass through the front door and when they did, I made my way to the bus stop that was only a short walk from the store along West Street. That time of the afternoon people were trying to make their way home from work and school, because of that the bus was crowded. That was the first time I had ever taken a bus without Mother. I was not worried because we had used the bus on many outings that we took, and I knew everything that was required if you wanted to reach you destination. The bus arrived at the stop by quarter past 4:00pm that afternoon, I boarded and sat halfway down the bus next to a man who was wearing overalls that had a strong smell of oil lingering to him. I imagined he might be a mechanic of some kind. The back seats of the bus were filled with students that were wearing the uniforms of the Saints Mary's College. They were mostly well mannered, they exchanged small talk with the occasional burst of laughter. The best part of taking the bus was sitting near a window and watching the homes go by. Some homes looked very grand and others looker worn and tired. I would often wonder about those homes, about the people that lived in them, did many people live there, how did they live their lives, where they happy or sad. I could not imagine living in such homes all alone, but I guess people do. But it is probably best not to think about it too much. The bus made many stops as we went. People got off and people got on. They were all very different people but every one of them, I can only imagine, carried the same goal. That being the goal of getting to their destination, that being work or home to loved ones that worry about them until they walk through their front door. It must be wonderful to have someone such as a lover that waits for you at home, worries for you and does not stop worrying until you get home. The bus turned onto Anzac Avenue and stopped when the lights turned red at the intersection of Drayton Road. I could see the Drayton Cemetery through the bus window. It was a very large cemetery that was spread out across a small hill that ran from Drayton

Road to Glenvale. The gravestones dotted the green grass that covered the hill like a green carpet and looked for all the world like grey soldiers charging over the hill into battle. The light turned Green, the bus turned to the right onto Drayton Road and pulled over to the bus stop that was near the main entrance to the cemetery. I departed the bus. The bus door had already closed and was moving away before I took my first step towards the entrance of the cemetery. Two large jacaranda trees stood either side of the main entrance gate their large branches swaying gently in the late afternoon breeze. Above the steel gate that was painted a deep blue were the words pronouncing the Drayton Cemetery. The faint sound of a mower cutting the grass could be heard from over the hill. I walked forward, the driveway gravel crunching under my feet. Grandmother was interned in the new section of the cemetery which was on the Southern side at the rear of the cemetery. I followed the road as it past the reception area and main carpark. At the end of the carpark was a narrow path with a sign to one side with a map outlining the different sections of the cemetery. I entered the path and made my way past the original section of the cemetery. The gravestones in that section were much older. Those headstones were adorned with carvings of angels and oversized crosses. Some head stones were covered in green moss which grew over the barely visible black writing declaring some of the graves to be more than a hundred years old. Some graves had couples interned side by side. I passed one that appeared to be set for a husband and wife but only one interned. One grave that lay near the pathway held the remains of a couple that had been interned since before the turn of the century and to the side lay a much smaller grave holding the remains of a baby girl. I gave it a passing glace, but I had my mind focused on what I had come to the cemetery to do. The path led me around the side of the hill to the new section of cemetery but before you could reach that section you had to pass through the cemetery rose garden. Along the path you had to pass under a large arbor. Growing over the arbor was a white climbing rose. The white roses grew in large bunches. The perfume filled your senses as you passed through it. The arbor then opened to the rose garden. Every rose of every color you could imagined was planted in the well-manicured garden. But it was not those that I had come to find. I stepped off the path and felt the soft grass sink beneath my feet. The rose perfume hung thickly in the air as I weaved my way through the bushes. I made my way to the rear of the garden as Mother, and I had done on our first visit to the cemetery after Grandmother's funeral. Mother has always had a strong sense of smell, Grandmother used to say, 'She had the nose of a blood hound' although I sometimes wonder whether that was God's compromise for not giving her the special gift. I was pushing her past the rose garden when she suddenly put the brake on her wheelchair on. 'I want a rose for her grave Abi!', she suddenly told me. The signs hammered into the earth along the path by the gardeners clearly stated that the roses where not to be picked. 'I don't care what the signs say Abi, your grand Mother is planted in the same ground so how could it be stealing if we put them there," she said before I turned the chair and started to push her through the rose bushes because deep inside, I knew she was. We made our way through the garden despite the wheelchair's wheels digging deeply into the lawn. I pushed hard as we went, Mother closed her eyes and sniffed the air, much like that blood hound I told you about earlier, even though I have only ever seen such a dog once. It was being led by a prison guard searching for an escaped prisoner in one of those old black and white prison escape movies. Without opening her eyes, she guided me to the rear of the garden, there we found one small red rose bush that seemed to be planted separate to the other roses in the garden. 'That's the one,' she said, excitedly pointing to the bush without even opening her eyes. 'What's so special about that one' I asked. 'Because it's been planted away from the others, almost forgotten, not as beautiful but it has the most beautiful overwhelming smell of all the roses in the garden, it is just like your grandmother, more special than the others but completely unseen.' Every time we went to the cemetery, we picked those red roses and placed them in a glass vase we placed in front of her head stone. I made my way through the roses, and I know it sounds stupid, but I had to know, I had to breath in that perfume, let my senses tell me the truth. The late afternoon sun was already on its way down and the light was fading when I knelt in front of that rose bush. It had not grown much since mother and I had found it, it was always stunted but always covered in the most sweat scented roses as if just for us or perhaps that was the reason the gardeners kept it in the rose garden in the first place. I cupped the biggest rose on the bush between my hands and held it to my nose. I greedily breathed in the rich perfume deep into my lungs. The perfume flooded across my senses along with it came the darkness flooding around the edges of my vision until I was consumed by it. I found myself standing again in the black water. Ripples poured out with every step as I struggled to balanced myself. The window before me cast no light into the darkness I found myself in, even though my eyes had to adjust to the brightness coming from that window. I stepped closer to the window and placed my hands onto the glass, it felt cold beneath my hands. My eyes were drawn to the picture on the wall. It seemed wrong somehow, changed. The colors were brighter, but they could not be. I scanned the path that led into the undergrowth for the faint red dots I thought I had seen before. They were there, bright red dots, something watching, waiting. It had all the time it wanted and would wait forever to have what it wants. In the center of the room sat another blonde-haired boy. He was playing peacefully with a wooden train set on the thick mat that covered the floor. As the boy played his lips moved. I could not hear the words although it was easy to imagine the train coming to life through the train sounds he must be making as it rolled along to its mystery destination. The boy was dressed in the same pajama bottoms. He suddenly stopped playing. His chest was pumping hard as his breathing quickened. He stared momentarily at the door then on his hands and knees he crawled quickly to the bed in the corner of the room and rolled himself underneath. The door flew open, and Mr Lard entered the room. He had an enraged look carved into his face. His eyes were large and bulging from their sockets. Saliva was running from the corner of his mouth. He had fresh looking blood covering the front of his suit and in his right hand he was carrying the thick leather belt. Immediately he knew where the boy was and with three large steps Mr Lard was at the bedside, lowered himself to one knee and reaching under the bed. The boy was pulled from his hiding place by his left arm and as he brought that belt down onto the boys back seven times, he screamed words at him slow and deliberately and even in silence I heard every one of them, 'look what you did to me!' I refused to look away even though every ounce of me wanted to. I Forced myself to look through paining eyes even though I wished I could be there for the boy. If I could be there, he would not have to be alone to suffer. I kept telling myself I did not want to look away while Mr Lard was beating the boy but movement above them caught my eye. An unnatural movement. The painting had changed again. It looked even brighter, more like a photo then a painting. To the side of the picture, I saw plants swaying as if a breeze was blowing inside that canvas. Their movements where so fluid and natural, but so unnatural that fear of the painting gripped at me with frozen fingers Something within the painting was moving forward, the undergrowth was being parted as it made its way through, then I saw the red dots again, they were burning like fire. The darkness around them was swirling, coming together, forming one form around the dots. The red dots moved forward from the shadows of the under growth. The darkness followed it. The darkness faded as it moved forward, I saw eyes, with the eye's I saw teeth. I felt the terror coming from the picture. It started deep inside my stomach chewing away at my insides like those hungry rats. They quickly crept up into my chest, then into my throat and erupted from my mouth. I screamed until I thought the boy and Mr Lard would hear me. I felt pressure on my shoulder, something was shaking me. 'Miss… Miss?" someone was asking from the darkness, over and over. The darkness then flashed away; a man was leaning over me. It was one of the cemetery gardeners, he had a thick heavy beard, and he had a look of concern in his eyes. He was asking if I was alright. My head was spinning. I sat up and did the first thing that came to mind, I lied, I told him I was fine. 'I don't want to sound awful Miss, but the gates are closing shortly,' he kept telling me, I got to my feet, told him I was fine again and made my way back to the bus stop. I caught the bus at the Drayton bus stop as the last rays of orange sunlight were disappearing on the Western horizon. I sat at the rear of the bus away from anyone who might think me peculiar and give me any unwanted attention. I had never been out this late before without Mother. I thought I would be alright if I just stayed away from the other passengers. I looked out through the bus window and watched the houses go by again. This time they were not empty. The families that call them home have returned. Some of the window's blinds are open and I can get a glimpse of inside the homes. Sometimes I see people inside and smile at that. I had never truly seen the city of a night-time before, and I think of everything that I have missed living alone with Mother in our sheltered life. It was beautiful and for a moment I longed to be a part of any one of those families, to be part of a normal family. I quickly brushed those thoughts off. I felt guilty, because having such thoughts would be some kind of betrayal to Mother. In a way it is betraying myself because it would be a lie to say I have never wished to be a bird and fly over the city of a night-time and see all the wonderful lights. The only confidence I have is in the knowing I would cry because of the beauty of it. I rested my head against the cold glass of the bus, it felt good. My eyes began to feel heavy again. I longed for home, to slip into my bed, but how would I sleep? The boy from the newspaper was in my head and every time I closed my eyes to sleep, I would see him. I tried to tell myself it was not the missing boy but the better part of me told me otherwise. It was around 7:20pm when the bus pulled into the West Street bus stop. I stepped off the bus and hurried as fast as I could go, knowing Mother would certainly be worrying. I almost fell once when my foot caught on a concrete lip. It took me another fifteen minutes to reach the large glass doors that opened to the foyer of our block of flats. I pushed the door open and rushed inside. Cigarette smoke filled the air inside, it made me nauseous. A man from the first floor was sitting on the first row of steps. A cigarette was drooping from his mouth, despite the large sign on the foyer wall stating no smoking was allowed. I paid him little interest, even though I could feel his eyes intensely staring at me. I rushed up the stairs past him. I took the stairs two at a time using my left hand on the handrail to help my ascent. I had just cleared the second floor when Himmler from unit 48 began to descend the stairwell. Behind him he was pulling the tow-along trolly. He stopped and watched me approaching. I slowed to a walk as I made my way past him. He diverted his eyes to the stairs. He was trying hard not to make eye contact. He passed me. I kept my gaze ahead of me, navigating the stairs without falling but studying him from the corner of my eye as I passed. He looked uninterested in the crazy girl madly racing up the stars. His eyes never moved as I passed but as his face disappeared from my view, I thought I saw the corner of his lip curl up in a sneer. I continued to the second-floor stairs, I stopped and peered over the edge of the handrail and watched Himmler disappear around the corner of the staircase. I continued up the staircase until I reached the third floor and stopped when I saw Mother in the hallway, a very concerned expression covering her face. The elevator door was open, she was about to wheel herself inside when she saw me enter the hallway. I knew she would be worrying terribly because she had her rosary beads rapped around her right hand. I grabbed the handles of the wheelchair and pulled it away from the elevator doors. 'What are you doing?' I asked, already knowing the answer. 'You have never been this late before, I was so worried, I wanted to go out and look for you,' she told me and even though I did not look I knew there were tears with what she said. 'You don't have to worry about me so much' I replied. 'Abigale May Price!' she said with a little dismay in her tone, I am your mother, I have always worried about you, and I always will worry about you.' 'I know… I am sorry, but I have a good reason.' 'Of course, you have a good reason, you are a good girl Abi, you wouldn't worry me without a good reason.' I pushed Mother back to our flat. She sat and listened contentedly as I told her about dreaming of Grandmother and my trip to the cemetery to visit her. Mother finished her tea and sat silently swirling the remainder of the tea in her cup as she often did when she was thinking. She stopped and looked at me. 'I always thought I was lucky to not be born with the gifts that your grandmother had. But always I have wished for it more so that you could not have been born with the burden of it.' I reached across and clasped my hands around hers. She looked directly into my eyes and said, 'What I do know for sure is that I cannot help you with what you see, and what I also learnt from your grandmother is that what you see cannot hurt you as long as you don't let it.' 'I'm always very careful when they come to me, but Grandmother seemed so real.' 'I think sometimes when it's quite I feel her presence also,' she said to me as she scanned the kitchen as if expecting to see a ghost, 'but maybe… just maybe, it's just the familiar things that you feel. I mean her voice, the way she laughed, all the things that we were used to her doing that we did not really take much notice of. I suppose you get used to these things when you have lived with someone for so long and only God knows how much I miss her too and there's nothing I wouldn't give to have her back.' We talked for what seemed forever. I wanted to tell her about the missing boy. The words lingered on my lips many times during our conversation, but the words never came. I have always told Mother everything and I know I could trust the advice she would give me. I am still not sure if it were because I thought she would believe me or not or maybe at that point I was struggling to believe it myself. The Reaper in the hallway suddenly bellowed making me jump a little. The time was two hours till midnight. Mother looked at me concernedly, 'You look tired,' she said. I agreed. I left the table and gathered up the teacups, rinsed them under the tap and placed them in the drying rack. Mother sat and watched me without saying a word. That task done I then wheeled her into her bedroom. I switched on the bedside lamp which only gave off a very dim glow. Mother never liked the darkness and always insisted the light be turned on and never turned off until she woke. I pulled the bed covers back and guided the chair alongside her bed. I then helped her from her chair and into the bed. I kissed her check gently and said good night.

TUESDAY

I went from room to room, turning off every light in the flat as I did. The flat suddenly felt dark and unknown. I stood still until my eyes adjusted to the darkness. I then instinctively negotiated my way through the kitchen then into the hall. The senser lights came on and I made my way to the bathroom to ran myself a hot shower. My eyes felt heavy. I entered the small bathroom that was across the hall from Mother's room. I opened the door where the darkness still dwelled. I reached in feeling for the light switch that was on the wall to my right. I found it with the tips of my fingers and switched it on. The light flashed on followed by the whirl of the exhaust fan as it spun into life. At the opposite end of the bathroom, I saw a woman staring back at me. Our bathroom was very small. Living in a flat did not allow for the luxury of open space. I could only imagine other bathrooms in the building were equally sized. The space allowed for what had to be done when you were there and little else. The minimal space did at time prove a challenge for mother's wheelchair. The floor was covered in white tiles. They had to be scrubbed on a regular basis to rid the room of the mould. It would creep into the grout between the tiles so quickly because the exhaust fan did little in the way of removing the steam from the room. The shower cubical was built into one corner of the room at floor level so Mother could easily access it without fear of falling. Inside the cubical the maintenance man had installed a seat so Mother could sit and shower herself without the chore becoming to tiring for her. Mother depended on my help of course. Getting from the wheelchair to the shower seat was the problem. Her legs are weak, but they can support her with the help of the handrail that runs along the wall of the cubical. It is always an ordeal for her, but I help her the best I can. I turned on the water and adjusted the temperature. The hot water running over my aching body was a welcome relief. The room was quickly engulfed with steam. On the far end of the bathroom above the hand basin, a large oval mirror was attached to the wall. My naked reflection stared back at me as I watched the steam cloud up its cold surface. It started at the bottom, creeping in like a ghostly fog. I watched until my reflection disappeared completely, and that girl disappeared. I felt alone. The bathroom was emersed with steam. I could see no further than the edge of the cubical. The sound of the exhaust fan working tirelessly in a vain attempt to extract the steam seemed to fade out when it disappeared in the gloom. I rested my head back on the white tiles that covered the cubical. I closed my eyes. I breathed the hot moist air deep into my lungs. I suddenly found it hard to breath. There was too much steam. I could feel moisture trickling down my throat with every breath. I quickly stood up and turned the shower off. The taps squeaked with every turn until the water pressure died. I stepped out of the cubical onto the cotton mat that had been placed in front of the cubical. Instead of my feet sinking into the thick cotton material I immediately felt the cold water beneath me and saw the familiar darkness. A boy was standing in the window. He was wearing the pyjama bottoms the first boy was wearing. I was certain he could not see me even though he was staring directly towards me. I do not know what people inside the window see when they look out. I can only assume it is their own familiar surrounds. He seemed transfixed by whatever it was he was seeing. I walked towards the window. The coldness from the water was creeping into my feet. I stood face to face with him. The only thing dividing us was the thin layer of glass. His eyes where a striking blue like the previous boy. He had recently had a haircut of a short back and sides style. His age was around seven the same as the other boy, but his face was rounder. He leaned forward as if to get a better look at what was outside the room. I touched the glass. I wanted to touch his face, but it had turned to see Mr Lard coming through the door. The leather belt was already in his hand. I did not watch as the boy was delivered the seven strikes from the belt. My attention was on the tiger that had emerged from the shadows beneath the undergrowth. Mr Lard then left the room leaving the boy laying on the floor. The seven welts had already begun to swell across his back, they looked red and angry. Tiny droplets of blood were trickling down his side, seeping from where the corners of the belt cut into his skin. I looked back to the picture. The tiger had not moved. It was watching, waiting. It still looked far off down the path. The sun shone brightly off its black and orange coat. It was standing still and silent like a house cat ready to pounce on a tiny bird that is playing in the bird bath. But the bird was not there this time, it was replaced by a boy that would make an even better meal. It focused all its attention on him until the man came back through the door and walked calmly back into the room. I watched the tiger watching him as he walked past the boy laying in the centre of the room and approached the bed. He scooped up the pillow. He turned towards me. A strange smirk made his mouth look lopsided. He carried the pillow by both ends and stood triumphantly over the boy, momentarily seeming to be fluffing the pillow. It was then that the reality of what was going to happen struck me like a thunder bolt. He then placed the pillow over the boy's head. He pushed down hard as if the boy was strong enough to put up a fight. The tiger watched. Seemingly relishing in the boy's misery. Then its mouth dropped open as if taking deep breaths, it threw its head back and gave off a silent roar. 'Yes… show me more,' I could imagine it saying. It lowered its head and grinned. I saw teeth, sharp teeth. I screamed until I thought my head would burst. I wanted to open the window, open the window and fight the man with all my strength. I had every intention of doing just that, but Grandmothers words came to me like a brick wall comes to a wayward bike rider, 'just ripples on a pond and I did not throw the stone.' I told myself over and over. When all the life had drained out of the boy's body and his tiny arms and legs had given their last movement in a desperate attempt to save himself, the man straightened and walked back to the bed. He placed the pillow back on the bed, he even fluffed it as if it were expecting to be used again shortly. I stood there, in the darkness, completely naked and that is exactly how I felt. Grandmothers' words were still echoing through my head as I watched the man leave the room and quickly return dragging something behind me. It was the tartan tow-along trolly. The exact same one I had seen Himmler from unit 48 using. He dragged the trolly to the boy's lifeless body. He then carefully unzipped the top cover and flipped it back to display the dark space inside. He then lent over the boy and braced him by his ankles. With little effort the boy was hanging from the man's hands above the trolly. The boy's arms and head went in first until he was up to the boy's midsection then he had to bend each leg to the knee to fit the boy inside the trolly. He then slid the zipper shut. Each zipper tooth entering the runner like a hungry mouth devouring them glutinously, then the boy was gone. The tiger watched all of this with a shrill look covering its face until the man left the room and shut the door behind him. Then it turned its attention towards me. I could not see its eyes clearly. At this distance they still appeared as red dots. They said to me, 'I can see you watching me,' I was certain, 'can you also see my teeth, come closer, you will see them better,' it then took a step forward and I took a step back in fright and fell. My back landed hard on the floor driving the wind out of my lungs with a whooshing sound. I lay there on the bathroom floor staring up at the exhaust fan. My head was spinning from the fall. I could feel a headache rushing its way in deep inside my head. The steam had cleared from the room. The exhaust fan was still chugging away. I got to my feet and left the bathroom turning off the light and exhaust fan as I went. I stepped into the hallway making my way to my room and without even putting on a night gown I slipped into bed.

WEDNESDAY

I woke to the smell of bacon drifting throughout the flat, the occasional clanking of cutlery and the kettle that let out its piercing scream. Mother was busy making breakfast and she sounded happy by the gentle tune she was humming to herself. I looked down to the bed cloths that were bunched up around my ankles. I must have discarded them during the night. The early morning breeze blowing in through my window was caressing my naked skin. I had slept right through the night, I felt good. My Spar uniform was neatly pressed and hanging from the doorknob where Mother had left it earlier that morning. I sat up just as the Blue Wren landed on my windowsill. Without paying me any attention he began his dance along the windowsill. The morning sun silhouetted him perfectly as if he were shone on by a stage spotlight. All he really needed was a top hat and a cane under his wing and he could have been Fred Astaire from one of those old black and white movies mother and I had once watched. Backwards and forwards he danced, perhaps for an audience only he could see. He looked so grand in his tiny blue vest. I could almost hear the music in my ears. I closed my eyes and listened. The crowd was silent as they watched the Wrens performance. They watched as if in a trance. He danced and sang like only a Blue Wren would know how and when he took his final bow the ordinance was in an uproar. I opened my eyes and saw Grandmother at the end of my bed, 'Aren't they the most magical things?" she said with a dreamily look in her eyes. 'Grandmother I….' I began. 'Hush now Abi,' she said holding up one finger, before the words had even got out of my mouth, 'there is nothing you can do for them, what's done is done, just like we talked about.' I did not realise I had begun to cry. 'All you need to worry about is that the beast knows, now hush because his partner has just arrived,' Grandmother added, and a look of excitement spread across her face. I turned back to the Blue Wren that was still dancing and holding Grandmother's attention. The Blue Wren had been joined by its mate, a much plainer looking bird that stood still on the windowsill while her mate danced around her. I turned back to Grandmother. I was in an empty room. I dressed, eat breakfast with Mother then made my way to work. Without fail I found Mother waiting at the door to say goodbye when I left. I think sometimes she gets lonely when I am gone. She would never tell me that of course. The flat can be a very lonely place when all you have is the radio for company and memories of loved ones that are gone. It is the quiet, it is the perfect place for long forgotten voices to hide and call out to you when you hear nothing else. I believe that is why she turns the radio up so loud, to drown out those voices. I said goodbye and made my way to work. I had just entered West Street when I saw the ambulance, then I saw the people gathered on the sidewalk. I walked closer, as I neared the crowd a police car arrived. I had to leave the foot path and make my way around them by walking across someone's front lawn. I then saw the dead dog laying underneath a blanket someone had placed over it. The police quickly left their vehicle and were approaching the crowd. As I passed the crowd one of the policemen was being bombarded with versions of what had happened. Before I had even past the crowd, I understood everything. The dog had been crossing the street and was struck by a passing car. The lady in the ambulance had stopped to help the injured dog and had been bitten on the arm by the injured animal. After the dog had bitten the lady, another car had stuck the dog and killed it. I guess who ever owned that dog was completely unaware their lives were changing drastically without them knowing it. I would have been devastated to see such a thing. I passed quickly and put it behind me, as best I could. I arrived at work and set about carrying the papers inside. Mr Spencer payed me little attention after his morning greeting, which consisted of a grumbled good morning after he had put out the displays then headed for the small kitchen that was at the rear of the shop to make himself a coffee. I ripped off the first of the blue straps and turned the paper over. The blond-haired boy that had been stuffed into that towa-long trolly was staring back at me. The boy's name was Chris Doolan. The paper said the boy had been snatched through his bedroom window and his parents woke to find the boy gone. His body had been found floating in a drain that flows into Murphy's Creek. After Chris Doolans body was recovered from that creek people were afraid as you would understand. The police were stirred up like a meat ants' nest after a child had deliberately ran over it. From behind the checkout counter, I saw police cars going backwards and forwards along West Street all day long. I finished stacking the papers and readied the checkout for the first customers to arrive. A steady flow of customers came in. I served each one uneventfully and cleaned and stacked shelves in between. At 12:30pm Mr Spencer told me to take my lunch. Queens Park was only a short walk down the street where you could sit at the tables in the shade trees and enjoy your lunch amongst the gardens When I arrived, there was only one couple sitting at the opposite end of the park. A boy and girl were playing on the swings. Next to the swings was a wooden climbing castle among other equipment. The boy was gently pushing the girl and their parents were watching them like hawks. I sat down on a concrete picnic table, underneath a giant pine tree. When I sat down, I felt the cool seep up from the concrete into my legs, even though my slacks. I placed my backpack on the table. In a side pocket, neatly rolled up, was a small blanket that Mother insisted I always place on the table before putting my food any were near it. 'The picnic tables are a petri dish of filth,' Mother had told me, and I tended to agree with her. I then started to take my lunch from the bag which consisted of sandwiches, juice, and fruit. I poured myself some apple juice into a small red cup and bit into my egg sandwich. It tasted good. I sat peacefully eating my lunch and studying the giant trees that grew within the park. They always made me feel small but somehow alive. The boy suddenly ran towards his parents, leaving the girl stranded on the swing. Her screams of disapproval filled the entire park. The man then walked across and lifted her out and placed her onto the ground. The girl then ran across and wacked the boy in the arm then ran off. The mother was then saying something to the father, and he threw his hands up in the air then sat back down at the picnic table again. I ate the last of my sandwiches down to the last piece of crust then washed that down with the remaining apple juice. I decided to head back to the store. I then packed my things back into my backpack and swung it over my left shoulder. I left the park and made my way back. I reached the automatic doors of the Spar store by thirty minutes past 1:00pm. I was not surprised when only the regulars came into the store that afternoon. Mostly the regulars and by that, I mean they come in seven days a week. Some come for the daily paper. Some buy cigarettes or a lotto ticket. Some even buy all three of those things. But as Mr Spencer says it is the regulars that keep the money coming in regularly. The afternoon had reached 3:30pm when Mr Spencer came out to the checkout carrying the little Sony wireless that always sits in the middle of the table in the store kitchen. Mr Spencers forehead looked as if a plough had travelled over it. The deep furrows running from his temple to the start of his nose immediately worried me. "Abigale…Abigale…" he was repeating over and over. He placed the black and grey radio on the counter. 'What is it?' I asked with concern. Something deep inside me knew exactly what he was going to say, but when he said it the rats that were already chewing away at my insides suddenly became ravenous. 'The police have found another dead child?' Mr Spencer turned the volume up and tilted his head toward the radio as if he were deaf. There were no customers in the store as we listened to a voice coming from the small radio telling us that Joe Summers small body had been pulled from a skip bin earlier that afternoon at a construction site on Ruthven Street. A builder was cleaning up after a job when the gruesome discovery was made. I tried hard to listen, but I could feel the darkness trying to creep its way across my vision. The voices then changed, we were listening to another man, a very deep voiced man who spoke with confidence. Other voices in the background threatened to drown out his voice. I guessed they were reporters firing questions at him. He briefed the reporters on their progress of finding the person or persons responsible and finished by calling for assistance from the public and advising anyone with information to please come forward. I then heard the policeman say he would answer one final question and a reporter asked if they knew how the boy had died. I did not sense any hesitation in his voice when he told the reporter that the cause of death was still unknown, but he could reveal that the killer seems to target blonde haired boys aged from 7 years to 10 years. A high pitch then erupted from the radio speaker. Mr Spencer was still listening, with his head turned to one side. I put my hands to my ears to fend off the sound. Mr Spencer was oblivious to what was happening. I reached out with my right hand to switch of the sound. I saw the light shine out from behind my hand, through my fingers and into my eyes. I was blinded by it. I closed my eyes. The scream of the radio was gone. I opened my eyes into darkness. I moved quickly across the black water to the window. Mr Lards task had already been completed. The boy lay lifeless in the middle of that room, but I barely noticed, even when he entered the room, bringing with him the drag-a-long trolly. I wanted to see the picture on the wall. The tiger had moved closer along the path. It was a very large tiger that towered over the undergrowth. The shine of its orange and black coat shimmered in the rays of sunlight that penetrated the canopy and brought life to the floor of the jungle. It was standing deathly still, watching Mr Lard going about the task of placing the boy inside the trolly. Its eyes followed him as he moved across the room dragging the trolly. He left the room closing the door behind him. The tiger took a step forward then concentrated its stare through the window towards me. Its eyes were mesmerising. I found it hard to look away. It opened its mouth revealing its teeth. It took in short sharp pants. It seemed to be smiling at me or a cunning sneer. 'Open the window and let me in,' the smile was saying, 'open the window and let me eat you,' was what those red penetrating eyes were really saying. The light flashed back when Mr Spencer turned the knob on the side of the radio killing the signal, Mr Spencer looked at me, 'I think we should close the store for the day,' then without saying anything else I helped him lock up the store and I made my way home.

THURSDAY

Mother has always taught me that a woman must have inner strength to survive the challenges that life throws at them. I know she is right because she survived Father walking out on her. She survived losing Grandmother. She survived all those years working at the dry cleaners and now she fights the sickness that is consuming her, even though in the end I know it will steal her away from me. She is a very strong woman, and on that day, I hoped I would have enough strength to do what I knew had to be done. But Inner strength is something I have always lacked. The strength to do something you never imagined possible or would even dare contemplate, but from here on in that choice was already made for me If I did not want to live with the pain of it for whatever remained of my life. The Reaper announced it was three hours past midday as I was making Mother her afternoon tea. It has been her afternoon ritual since she became ill to listen to the afternoon news. To know what was happening outside her walls. I was busy setting the small table next to her chair with her tea and cream biscuits that she always insisted on and was about to turn on the radio when I heard the thumping sound of the tug-a-long trolly coming up the star well. I switched on old Zenith radio that sat on a small table beside the sofa. The radio had belonged to Grandmother and used to be in her room, but Mother thought it best to use it then leave it sit silent. The familiar sound of the ABC News broadcast erupted from the speaker. I then parted the curtains enough so the afternoon sun could filter through the windows. Mother was shifting in her chair trying to get comfortable. I retrieved a small cushion from the sofa, puffed it and squeezed it down the back of her chair. Mother said that was much better and I left her to listen to the news. Thursdays were important days in the flats, not just for us but for everyone who lived there. Thursday was rent day. Since Mother and I moved into the flat with Grandmother we knew the routine. Every Thursday afternoon was Mr Fawley's designated day to bang on each and every door of the block, that is the flats that were already late with their payments. He would start on the bottom level and work his way to the top. Times were hard on most people, and he seemed to bang on a lot more doors than he used to. When the banging started, I returned to Mother and adjusted the volume knob to drown out the noise. I then opened our front door. I held it open slightly so I could watch as Mr Fawley entered our hallway. He moved along banging on doors as he went. He banged on flat 41 and 53. He thumped on the doors until his fist must have ached then yelled out a well-rehearsed curse. Before he was even halfway up the stairwell to level three, I had left our flat and was descending the stairwell to the bottom level. On the bottom floor was Mr Fawley's flat where he lived alone. I have never seen inside his flat and do not wish to. But if it is anything like his personal hygiene then it must be in a state of filth. I reached the bottom floor, there was no one in sight except for the open door on the opposite side of the foyer which was Mr Fawley's office. I had been in that office a number of times with Mother to pay our rent. It was a small room with a counter dividing the room into two sections. On one end of the counter sat an old cash register that Mr Fawley always used. Mother once told me it is there for looks alone and the money would never see the darkness inside that register, even though I doubt the money is hidden inside his mattress like Mother says. I immediately saw the object of my mission, the large key rack behind the counter. Around the key rack where old black and white pictures. I believe they were Mr Fawley's parents, the original owners of the flats. I scanned the foyer one last time then entered the office. I moved with hast. The stench of cigarettes was overwhelming. It seemed to be imbedded in everything in the small office. From the plaster board of the walls to the worn red carpet that covered the floor and every other room in the building. I went behind the desk and searched the board until I found Key 48. I snatched it off the hook and stuffed it into the pocket of my Spar uniform. I left the office and waited at the bottom of the stairwell and listened for Mr Fawley. I could hear his loud cursing echoing down from above like an angry God from the heavens. He was now on the upper levels. I took the steps two at a time and had not reached the second floor when I could feel his familiar stare cutting through me like heat through ice. I stopped and looked up; Mr Fawley was looking down at me from the fourth floor. I hurried as fast as I could while looking up to see if he were there. He was gone. I reached the last stair of the second floor when I felt a hand clasp around my wrist. It happened so quickly my head spun, and I was against the wall with Mr Fawley pinning my arms tightly. He put his face up close to mine.

He was sweating and his eyes were blood shot from all the yelling. 'Why are you working, girl?' he asked, with each word came the stench of cigarettes. 'If you were mine, you would never have to work.' He released my left hand and I felt it touch my upper thigh. 'Your mothers going to be dead soon enough, I could take care of you,' I felt the hand go higher, closer to the flat key that was in my pocket. 'Real good care,' he added and brought his face against mine. I felt his tongue run along my cheek, it felt warm and wet and sickening. His unshaven face scratched my cheek. He made a slight sound of approval as that disgusting thing slid across my cheek, I then lifted my knee as hard and as high as I could. I felt it was a feeble attempt to fight him off but the look in his eyes filled me with some sense of victory. His eyes immediately opened as if they were going to fall out and bounce all the way down the stair well. An agonizing look, one that I will never forget instantly covered his face. I am sure it was the pain that was shooting up his body like an electrical current, even though I like to think it was the thought that I had got the better of him. He released me from his grip and stumbled backwards clutching at his groin and I ran down the hall toward our front door as fast as I could. I made it through our front door as the first curse came hurtling after me, followed by others as I closed and locked it. I stood there with my back against the door listening to him cursing me with the biggest smile on my face I could ever remember having and from deep within me I felt a chuckle come up from my stomach. I leaned against our front door and found myself laughing harder than I can remember doing so before. I was laughing so hard that Mother called out from listening to the news to see what had happened. I walked into the living room to let her know I was alright. She gave me a funny look because I was still chuckling. It was a small victory, but I am sure it helped give me the strength to do what I was about to do.

FRIDAY

Mr Fawley had long since disappeared from the hall when I found myself standing in front of flat 48. I will not say I was not scared; I was terrified. My stomach felt as if someone had buried their fingers deep inside and was squeezing my insides tight. My hands trembled as I slid the key into the door. The mechanism clicked effortlessly when I turned the key. I am still not sure what I was expecting to find and to say I was surprised when I found the flat to be completely normal as if I were in our own would be correct. But what should a killer's flat look like? I stepped inside and closed the door behind me. It is funny how you expect things to be a certain way. I guess I expected to see the type of killers flat that you would see in a movie or read about in a storybook. Mounted animals such as in the Bates Hotel or ghosts in the hallways of the Overlook Hotel. When I entered that flat, I did not find dead bodies decorating it or a room filled with pictures and newspaper clippings like a trophy room full of momentous. When I opened the door and stepped inside, I found every light in the flat was on. It was warm and inviting. I closed the door gently behind me, not wanting to announce the fact I was in the flat should anyone else reside here. Instantly the smell I smelt when I first met Himmler in the Spar store filled my head. I then saw the sources of the aroma. Scented candles were burning on a solid timber table in the centre of the living room. I then saw the picture frames that hung from the walls. In each frame were old black and white pictures of a man, woman, and a small boy. Each picture the same as the last. Beside the woman a man stood. He was wearing a suit for the happy occasion of taking a family portrait. The lady had a very pleased smile on her face and the boy looked as if that was the happiest day of his life. The man I could not tell his expression because his face had been removed from the picture I was looking at and every other picture on those four walls. Someone had painstakingly cut out the face in every picture. The furniture that decorated the living room looked handmade and expensive. On the floor lay the thick red carpet that lay all throughout the building. I made my way to the door that led through to the hallway. I knew exactly where the door lead because the layout of the flat was exactly the same as ours. I stepped into the hallway. At the end of the hall was a door that would normally lead to Mothers room. Two doors lay to the left, one was the bathroom and the other used to be Grandmothers room. The door I was looking for was to the right. I approached it and placed my hand onto the brass doorknob. It felt cold as I would expect. I turned the doorknob, the door cracked open emitting light that seemed brighter than the light the overheard hallway light was emitting. I stood there momentarily. A thin ray of light shone out the cracked door and across my arm. I felt the warmth and somehow it felt overly inviting, it was calling me to come inside. I listened to it and pushed the door open further. The light blinded me. It was like staring into a spotlight. I placed my left hand over my eyes to protect them, but the light only lasted momentarily, and it faded away as if someone had turned a dimmer switch. Right away I saw the red carpet that ran from the living room, through the hallway and wound its way carelessly into the bedroom like blood coursing through a vein. It was the room I had seen through the window. I stepped inside. I walked to the centre of the room and stood on the rug the boy's lifeless body had been laying on. It was exactly as I had seen it. The bed was in one corner with the teddy bear propped up against the pillow. The bookshelves and wallpaper with the drummer boys drumming their far away music. In the centre of the wall, I saw the picture. It was no longer a painting. It was clear and glossy as if looking through a window right into that jungle and there was the tiger. It had moved closer; it was hunched like it was going to pounce on some unexpected pray. I found myself tranced by its fierce red eyes as if they were drawing me in. 'Come closer,' they called, 'close enough for me to pounce.' I felt them burning right through me. I closed my eyes breaking the connection. I turned my head away desperately trying to ignore it. Something then caught my eye through the window. I stepped closer. It looked like a horse. I put my hands against the glass of the window. My legs felt weak and for a moment I felt panic creeping up my throat threatening to choke me. I then understood what the boy was looking at through the window. Through the window the city was gone. Concrete buildings replaced with wooden houses. Bitumen roads replaced with dirt. To the left of my view, I saw a horse and cart loaded with milk cans slowly making its way along the street. A man was sitting on the wagon guiding the horse with two loosely held reins. From his mouth hung a pipe. With each breath smoke billowed from his mouth past his thick moustache.

I looked across the tops of the houses to where I knew tall concrete buildings, filled with offices and other businesses, should have been. Those buildings are normally filled with people going about their everyday lives like ants in a nest. Their one purpose to work and be productive. But that productivity was gone along with the buildings, replaced with towering eucalyptus trees and others I do not really know. The cart disappeared out of my site. I looked down to the front of our flats to where I like to sit and gaze at the stars of a night. The large maple trees that were planted along the verge were gone as was the wooden seats. In fact, the concrete drains that bordered the verge and carried torrents of water during summer storms had disappeared and were now large puddles of dirty water. I then heard a click from the front door breaking me from my trance. I hurried from the room closing the bedroom door behind me. The door to the living room was closed as I had left it. I opened the door that would be our bathroom. The room was filled with darkness and silence. The exhaust fan did not come to life. I knew even if I could see my reflection at the other end of the room there would be something wrong with it. I pushed the door shut and held the door handle down hard so the bolt would not latch, and I could hold the door open a crack and not be seen. Using only my right eye I focused through the thin crack of light as the door from the living room opened and Himmler came through dragging behind him the tow-a-long trolly. He entered the hallway and closed the living room door behind him. I watched him coming down the hallway with the same strained expression on his face and the axil bent from the weight of what I knew would be in the trolley. He passed by me without glancing sideways.

His mind was focus on his evil deed. He entered the bedroom. I saw the light pass over him like he was passing through a waterfall. The light hurt my eye, tears welled there, but I refused to close it and staring through that light burnt like fire, but I would not close my eye because it hurt, I would not even blink. When the light faded away Himmler had disappeared, and Mr Lard now stood in the doorway. I then understood. Inside the room time has not changed, inside the room he becomes someone else. Mr Lard dragged the trolly into the room and placed it on the rug in the middle of the room then turned and closed the bedroom door. I then slipped through the bathroom door, made my way through the living room and out the front door.

THE END DAY.

I gently closed the door to my room so not to announce my presence inside my room to Mother. With my index finger I clicked the small latch under the handle locking myself in just to be sure. The Reaper announced that it was 6 hours to midnight. Mother would not leave the living room for dinner for another hour. I laid down on my bed, put my arms across my chest and closed my eyes. I squeezed them as hard as I could and concentrated on the window. I knew that that was the moment I had to give everything I had. Even though Grandmother had told me to never open the window it is what had to be done and there would be no going back once I did. I had never before willed myself into the darkness. I knew I could, but I was usure what to expect. I focused on the darkness behind my eye lids. The found the light came quickly. First like a far-off candlelight or even a firefly. Then as if the darkness were on fire it swirled in a blinding mass that quickly formed into the familiar window. It travelled at a frightening speed towards me. It stopped a short distance from me with the light I had come calling to me. I felt the cold creeping up from my feet. I leaned forward and saw my reflection in the water. I then saw ripples spreading out in front of me. Without realising I was moving toward the window. I saw movement in the room as I neared. A boy was alone in the room. I reached the window as he approached the glass and staired out. His expression changed when he reached the window. A look of bewilderment was etched into his face. I knew what he was seeing, and I wanted to tell him not to look. But even for such a young boy he knew what he was seeing was wrong. I put my hands up to the glass to try and reassure him, to comfort him. His face was so innocent. Too young to have sinned or lied or hurt anyone. His face was one of purity before the trouble that would eventually be delivered to him in the form of life. Movement behind the boy caught my eye. I looked over his thin shoulders and saw the tiger, it was panting in deep controlled breaths. The tiger was watching me. Its cold stare shook me from my focus on the boy. I raised my right hand toward the latch in the centre of the window frame. The tigers' eyes followed my hand. The tiger grinned. A look of delight seemed to spread across its face. It knew what I was going to do. Like feeding time at a zoo, it knew what was coming. I could not let that stop me. I released the latch and pulled open the window. The boy stumbled backwards in surprise until he was standing on the edge of the mat. I lowered myself through the window and stood in front of the boy. I knelt down and looked into his eyes. I told him not to be afraid and that he would have to be braver than he through he could be because Mr Lard was going to come through the door at any moment. That moment came. The brass doorknob turned. We watched as the door opened and we saw Himmler standing in the doorway looking at us with a confused look on his face. The look quickly turned to one of rage as he stepped through the doorway and the light flooded across him like that waterfall. In that thin ray of light, the old man melted away in an instant and reformed as he stepped into the light of the room like a moth crawling from its cocoon. Mr Lard now stood in the doorway. His expression changed from one of fury to the cold grin he always seemed to wear. He stopped and closed the door behind him. 'My boy said he thought he saw something in your eyes that day at the store, I did not believe him,' he said stepping closer to us. The boy wrapped his arms around me, and I could feel his tiny body shaking against mine. 'An admirer perhaps' he said stepping closer. He stopped before reaching the mat. 'Perhaps you should wish to join me. My boy does not have the stomach for it, I tried to correct him, but he is a very strong-willed boy.' My heart was pounding in my chest. I wanted to scream for fear my own bravery had reached the end of it tether. I looked toward the window; Mr Lard knew what I had in mind. I scooped up the boy and rushed towards it as fast as I could. If I could just reach the window, I could push the boy through, and he would be safe, but I barely reached the window before I felt two hands fall onto my shoulders. The hands spun me around and shoved me across the room and we both went crashing into the wall The air burst from my lungs on impact. I saw dark edges creep in around my vison. I told myself I cannot pass out. The boy hit the wall headfirst knocking him unconscious, blood was running from a cut to his forehead. A loud crash came from beside me. I turned and saw the jungle picture on the floor leaning against the wall. When we hit the wall, the impact had shaken it from its fixture. The glass that protected the picture had exploded across the room like a thousand diamonds across the red carpet. Straight away I caught the smell of trees and rotten vegetation, but the strangest thing is I thought I felt a gust of fresh air suddenly in the room. I looked down at the boy, he was still unconscious. I reached across and grabbed him by his arms and pulled him toward me. I hugged him against my body with determination Mr Lard was not going to have him. Mr Lard stood watching as I did this, 'you're not having him,' I spat through clenched teeth. My head ached with each word. The darkness was still chewing away at my vision, but I would not allow myself the easy way out by passing out. I watched Mr Lard watching me and I do not know how it was possible, but his grin seemed to widen. 'Why that one?' he asked looking confused, 'my boy will bring others.' 'Your son?' "Of course, you don't see the resemblance?' 'The old man is your son... how?' I asked, more myself then Mr Lard. 'I died in this room and now it is my prison,' he said as he began to remove his tie, he looped it over his head and discarded it onto the floor then undid his shirt. Underneath the red patch was a hole, a hole perfectly cut there. 'I was only saying goodnight, after correcting him of course. I pulled him close like any loving father would and had no idea my son had hidden a knife inside the teddy bear before he sank it into my heart.' 'Correcting... you were beating him!' 'No!' he said back, 'I was a good father, I loved him, I took care of him. I still do.' 'You made his life hell' 'I made him what he is. He knows the kind of children I like, and he gets them for me, and I correct them.' 'Because you can't beat him anymore.' 'That right.' I stared at him with all the intensity my tiring eyes could command and all the rage my body could hold, 'you take children like your son, you're still abusing him,' I yelled at him. Then I saw the smile fade from his face. His mouth screwed up in anger his eyes firmly fixed on his target, he rushed across to the bed and snatched the bear from the pillows and pushed his hand into the hole in the bears back. When he pulled his hand free, he was clasping a knife. He threw the bear back onto the bed. Rage had consumed him. His face was carved from pure hatred. At that moment I knew what was coming. I would not fight it; I had no fight left. If I were going to die, I would die with the knowledge that I did everything I could to help the boy in my arms. He lunged forwards towards me across the mat with the knife held high. I closed my eyes and hoped I would slip into unconsciousness before the blade cut through my flesh. Nothing came. I opened my eyes and saw Mr Lard stopped on the edge of the mat. He was staring into the broken picture on the floor. His expression changed from one of hatred to one of fear. I could not see what he was seeing and somewhere deep inside me did not want to see. Mr Lard stepped backwards, the word 'No' escaped his lips. I watched the picture frame. Something was coming closer as Mr Lard stepped backwards. I could not see what Mr Lard was seeing. I could only see the side of the heavy wooden picture frame. Then I saw a large orange and white paw come out of the frame. Another paw appeared. They were clawing at the wooden frame trying to pull itself through into the room. More of the front legs came through the frame. I saw long claws digging into the red carpet to use as leverage as it climbed out. Then I saw a muzzle covered in long thick whiskers burst from the frame. Deep bellied growls bellowed from its throat with every breath. Two giant paws were now firmly on the floor. Mr Lard moved further back until his back was against the wall. The tiger pulled itself forward until the first of its hind legs were through the picture frame. The tiger was enormous. It glanced sideways at myself and the boy. It sneered at us with a low acknowledging growl then quickly returned its attention to Mr Lard. The tigers' hind legs now rested on the edge of the picture frame and with a slight forward movement the tiger was in the room with us. The tiger glanced sideways at myself and the boy again. Its lips pulled back to display its large teeth then a low pitch growl was thrown at us as if displaying a warning. It then returned its attention to Mr Lard. He was holding the knife out in front of him, which seemed to bemuse the tiger as it stepped closer hunching itself down as if ready to pounce. Mr Lard then broke from the wall and rushed towards the open window; the tiger pounced after him. Mr Lards head went through the window followed by his upper body and instantly it changed back into Himmler. The Tiger pounced sinking its large teeth into Mr Lards upper thigh. Himmler screamed in pain. The tiger pulled backwards on Mr Lards leg, but Himmler was too old and week to pull himself free of the tiger. Mr Lard clutched desperately onto the window frame as the tiger continued dragging him backwards. His clawed fingers scrapped across the window frame, and he landed heavily onto the carpeted floor. I pulled the unconscious boy hard against my body as I watched helplessly. My head was spinning, and I am not even sure what I saw that day was even real, but I am probably the best judge of what is real and what is not given that most people would not believe what I see on a daily basis. But out of all the pain and misery that Mr Lard and Himmler caused was that the tiger was probably the best one to dish out a justice of some kind if you choose to call it that. I leaned back against the wall and watched as the tiger dragged Mr Lard towards the picture frame. Mr Lard screamed all the way and what has etched itself into my memory the most is the look he gave me just before his fingers that were clutching onto the edge of that picture frame gave out. I waited until Mr Lards screams died out. I gently laid the boy onto the carpet, got to my feet, and went to the picture. The tiger and Mr Lard were gone. I think and still I am not sure but far off in the distance I thought I could see the undergrowth moving where the tiger was still dragging him. I climbed back through the window, latched it again and woke up in my bedroom. My body was aching, and my head hurt but I willed myself back to flat 48. I scooped up the boy in my arms and carried him back to our flat and into our living room. I gently laid him out onto the sofa. Mother actually got to her feet in astonishment at seeing me carrying the boy. I helped her back to her chair. 'What have you done Abi?' she asked looking up at me with tears in her eyes, 'you must tell me,' her voice was firm, but her body was shaking. My legs then stated to feel weak. I sat down on the edge of the sofa and my strength left me and I cried harder than I have before and since. Mother did not try to stop me. She said you have to open the door to let pain out and if you shut the door before it has left it will eat you up eventually. I then told Mother everything and when I was done, she just sat there staring at the boy. I had seen her like that before when she was deep in thought. 'You should have told me Abi, but I understand why you did not. You have more courage than I have ever had, and I dare say your grandmother as well, but she would be very proud of you. Now we need to take care of the boy.' Mother watched from our front door as I carried the boy to the night watchman's door, once there, laid him out comfortably and knocked on the door. The night watchman discovered the boy and called an ambulance. It was on the front page of the Chronicle the very next day as I laid out the papers in the paper rack at the Spar store. The missing boy had been found safe and well. To my knowledge he had no memory of what he went through so could not tell the police anything, which was a good thing. The Newtown Killer, as he had become known, was never found and Himmler was never heard of again. Mr Fawley had that room cleaned out and a new family lives there now with no knowledge of what happened. The picture now hangs on my bedroom wall. I went back to flat 48 and collected it. I had a new piece of glass fitted to protect the picture and perhaps keep things from getting out. Slowly but surely life returned to normal. I am sure one day I will go back to that window and when I look inside, I will still see the picture laying on the floor and I would be certain that from the undergrowth of that jungle the tiger would be watching and waiting, it's hunger not yet satisfied, but for now it is caged on my bedroom wall. I guess that is a good way to end a journey and to start another, sitting her under the stars. The clouds have opened, and the night is beautiful. I feel stronger and richer than I have ever felt before. I have made new friends and look forward to making more. I have found new paths that lead in all directions and for the first time I am free to choose which path I take, and, in the end, Grandmother was right I am much stronger than I ever believed I could be.

-THE END-